THE ADVENTURES OF

Gary & Harry

A TALE OF TWO TURTLES

STORY BY LISA MATSUMOTO

ILLUSTRATION BY MICHAEL FURUYA

Published by *Lehua, Inc.* Honolulu, Hawaii

Printed and bound in Korea

All inquiries should be addressed to:
Lehua Inc.
P.O. Box 4
'Aiea, Hawai'i 96701

5 7 9 10 8 6 4

ISBN# 0-9647491-4-9

Library of Congress Control Number: 2006932567

Book design: Darryl Furuya

Acknowledgments
Howard Furukawa
Betty Furuya
Seizo Furuya
SueAnn Goshima
Ann Hudgins
Jon Lucich
Jennifer Matsumoto
Yukimasa Matsumoto
Jim Maragos
Mei Nakano
Stanley Nakano
Stacey Naki
Lori Nasu
Maile Sakamoto
Zan Shinmoto
Leigh Sturgeon
Randy Sturgeon
Genny Wilson

For my sisters Lori and Leigh
Thank you for your love, wisdom and support.   Lisa

For Cobi & Cameron
Just because.   Uncle Mike

Deep in the sparkling sea,

Gary the green sea turtle and his best friend

1

Harry the hawksbill turtle played in their ocean home.
Each day they would swim to the surface and happily dive beneath the waves.

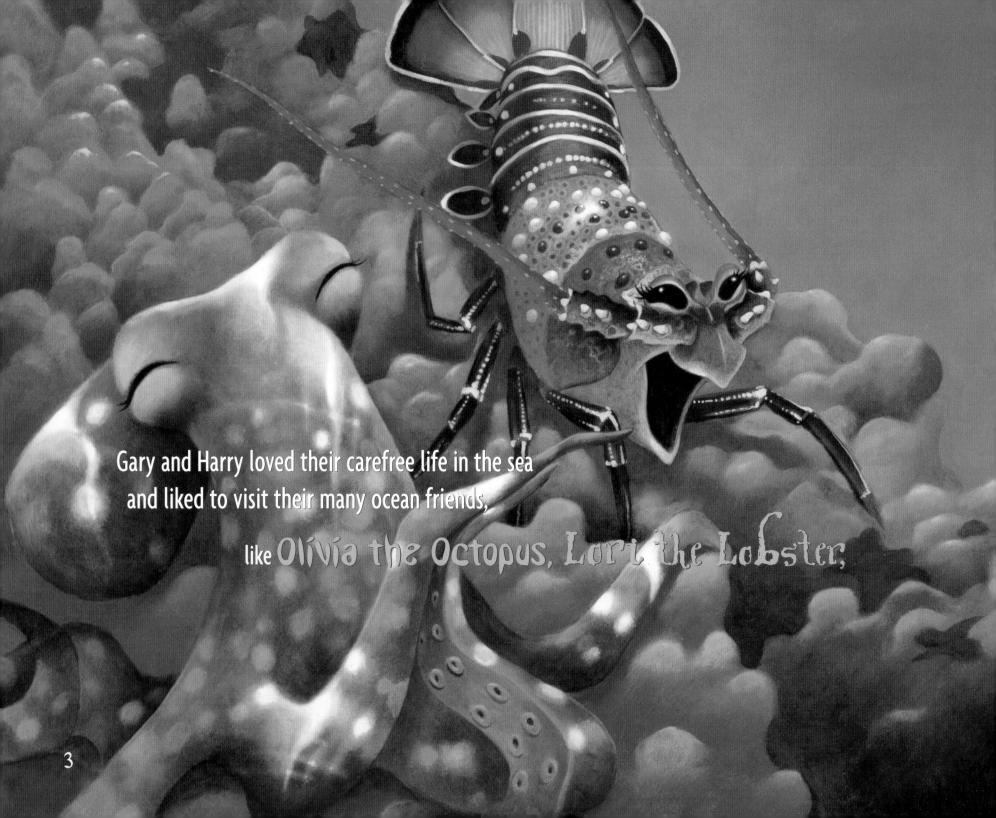

Gary and Harry loved their carefree life in the sea
and liked to visit their many ocean friends,

like Olivia the Octopus, Lori the Lobster,

3

and even **Herman, the grumpy old hermit crab,** who was really nothing but a big "softy" under that crusty old shell.

4

5

For Gary and Harry, each day was a great underwater adventure.
Some days they would explore
deep into dark underwater caverns.

7

Other days they would search for long lost treasures buried
deep in the hulls of old sunken ships.

When they wanted a good laugh, they would visit
the crazy clown fishes who performed in Harold Harlequin Shrimp's
Spectacular Sea Circus!

10

One day after their morning adventure, Gary and Harry were **especially hungry.**

As always, it was difficult deciding what to have for lunch since they had very different tastes in food. "How about a salty seaweed salad made of fresh algae?" Gary suggested.

"Algae?! Yuck!"

Harry replied making a face.
"I'd rather have a nice tasty jellyfish!"

12

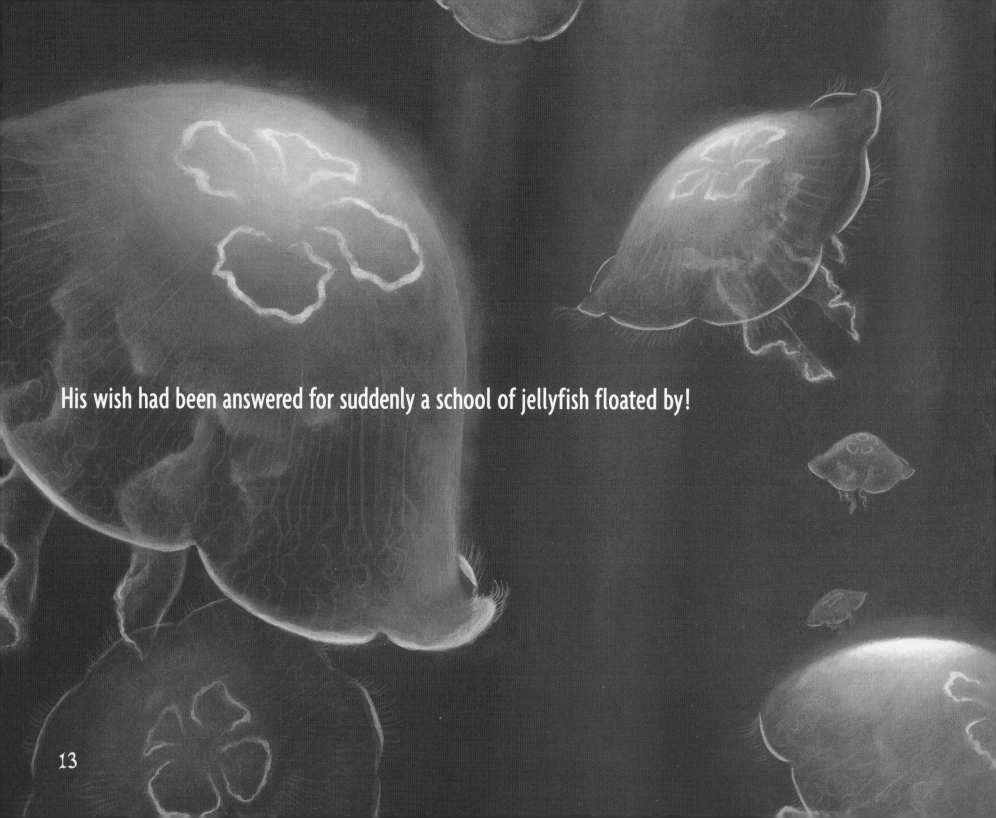

His wish had been answered for suddenly a school of jellyfish floated by!

"Wow! Look at all those jellyfish!"

14

Harry quickly swam to the largest one and swallowed it in ...

one big gulp!

Gary expected to hear a satisfied "Ahhh",
but instead Harry responded with a terrified...

16

Harry was gasping and choking! That was no jellyfish he had swallowed,
it was a plastic bag! Harry knew many sea turtles had died
from choking on plastic bags, but he never once thought it would happen to him!

Harry desperately tried everything to remove the plastic bag, but it just wouldn't come out! His life flashed before him!

Luckily, Gary had just completed his turtle safety class, and by using
the Heimlich maneuver, the plastic bag flew right out from Harry's throat!

"Whew! That was close!" Harry said while catching his breath.
"How did a plastic bag get in the ocean anyway?!"

"How else?" Gary answered, the humans."

"Well, they need to be more careful to keep their trash out of our homes!"
Harry said angrily. Gary couldn't agree with him more.

Suddenly Harry's stomach rumbled.

All the excitement worked up his appetite. "Well, I'm starving!" He told Gary.

"Let's get lunch!" Just then a beautiful jellyfish floated by. "Look Harry! Just what you asked for."

21

Lunch!

22

After what Harry had been through, suddenly jellyfish
didn't seem very appealing.

"I'll pass on jellyfish for awhile,
maybe I'll try one of those salty seaweed salads."

Gary's face quickly lit up. "Well, I know the perfect place to go!"
he said excitedly.

And with a flick of their flippers

they quickly dove through the crystal blue water, eager to
enjoy a nice, delicious, relaxing lunch!

The End.

26

Pacific Green Sea Turtle
Photo © Jim E. Maragos

The pacific green sea turtle weighs up to 400 pounds and is primarily vegetarian, eating algae and seaweed growing underwater on coral reefs and on rocks close to shore. The upper shell is dark with olive or gold flecks. They are named for the green color of their body fat. There once were tens of millions of green sea turtles around the world. Now there may be fewer than 200,000 mature females. The pacific green sea turtle is a threatened species. Their numbers have declined due to predation by tiger sharks, loss of nesting sites due to coastal development, captured for their meat and shells and entanglement in nets and fishing gear. Recently many green sea turtles have developed tumors which affect them so they eventually can't see, move and breathe.

Pacific Hawksbill Turtle
Photo by David R. Schrichte

The hawksbill turtle is named for its sharp beak-like mouth. The hawksbill is a medium-sized turtle weighing around 270 pounds and is predominantly mottled brown with dark and light spots and streaks. They are known for their beautiful shells often referred to as "tortoise shell". Although illegal in most countries, many turtles are still exploited for fashion jewelry. Hawksbill turtles feed on sponges, sea anemone and assorted invertebrates, unfortunately, Styrofoam and plastics have been mistaken for food. The pacific hawksbill turtle is a critically endangered species with fewer than 30 nesting hawksbills in the Hawaiian Islands today. Historically humans have been the greatest predator of this sea turtle, killing it for its shell, driving it almost to extinction. Today most nesting populations are declining due to the destruction of their nesting habitats. Dogs, cats and mongoose also eat eggs and hatchling sea turtles. As adults the only other natural predator other than humans are sharks.

Day Octopus
Photo © Jim E. Maragos

Octopus are mollusks and are closely related to squid and cuttlefish. Unlike other mollusks such as snails and clams, octopus do not have a hard shell, and therefore must depend on other defenses for survival. They have large complex brains and have been shown to problem solve and learn from experience. They are also able to change their skin color to blend with their surroundings. When in danger, the octopus releases a cloud of black ink to distract and blind its predator then makes a fast escape. Day octopus are found on shallow reefs and are most active during the day when they feed on shrimp, lobsters and crabs.

Banded Spiny Lobster
Photo by David R. Schrichte

Like other crustacean, the spiny lobster has a hard external skeleton (exoskeleton) and jointed limbs. The spiny lobster has a spine-studded shell and long antennae but unlike other lobsters, it has no large front claws. It gets its name from the strong, sharp, forward curving spines that cover its antennae and shell. During the day, spiny lobsters are often found hiding under ledges or in caves and emerge at night to hunt for food. Being scavengers of the reef, they feed on reef invertebrates and animal carrion.

Anemone Hermit Crab and Hermit Crab Anemone
Photo by David R. Schrichte

Unlike other crabs, hermit crabs do not have a hard shell completely covering their bodies. To protect themselves they live in the discarded shells of other animals. The anemone hermit crab is a species of hermit crabs, which attaches sea anemone to its shell. The anemone protect the crab from enemies, especially the octopus, which eats hermit crabs but is very sensitive to anemone stings. The anemone may also help camouflage the hermit crab. In return, the anemone receives a free ride around the reef. By riding from place to place on top of a crab, the anemone is able to get scraps of food it might not have been able to get on its own.

Harlequin Shrimp
Photo by David R. Schrichte

The harlequin shrimp is a crustacean and like its lobster and crab relatives, it has an exoskeleton and jointed limbs. It is one of the most stunning shrimps with its bright colored spots, which helps it to blend in with its surroundings. The harlequin shrimp, which grows to 2 inches in length, feeds solely on seastars (starfishes). After locating its prey by smell the tiny harlequin shrimp crawls under the seastar and flips the star over to feed on its vulnerable underside.

Clownfish
Photo © Jim E. Maragos

Clownfish, also known as anemonefish, make their home among sea anemone. Unlike other fishes, clownfish are immune to the stinging cells of the anemone's tentacles. The relationship between the clownfish and anemone is symbiotic, benefiting them both. The anemone's stinging tentacles provides protection for the clownfish while the clownfish protects their anemone host by chasing away animals such as the butterfly fish, which often feed on anemone. Clownfish can be found in shallow water reefs and feed on algae, plankton and small crustacean.

Jellyfish (Sea Jelly)
Photo Waikiki Aquarium

Jellyfish, or sea jellies, are not fish, but are invertebrates (animals without backbones) and have lived in the Earth's oceans for over 650 million years. They are relatives of sea anemone and corals and vary in size, shape and color. Jellies are made up of salt, protein and 95% water and have no eyes, brain or heart. They travel by drifting or by using their umbrella-like bodies to propel them through the water. Jellies may be graceful and elegant creatures, but they possess painful stinging tentacles, which are still able to sting even after the animal is dead. Jellies are carnivores and do not actively hunt for food, but passively catch their prey as it drifts by.

Marine Debris
Photo by David R. Schrichte

Marine debris is any object found in the marine environment that does not naturally belong there. Most common are: plastic, glass, rubber, metal, paper, wood, cloth and discarded nets. 80% of all marine debris comes from land-based activities. The sources of all marine debris are people. People dump more than 14 billion pounds of garbage each year into the world's oceans. Plastics are especially dangerous as marine creatures ingest or are entangled in them. Thousands of marine mammals die from entanglement or ingestion of marine debris each year.

How you can help

• Volunteer for beach and stream clean ups.

• Recycle your six pack rings, aluminum cans, newspapers, plastics and glass. Before recycling your six pack rings, cut through the loops to prevent entanglement of wildlife should the ring wind up in the environment.

• Do not release helium filled balloons into the air. Many of these balloons end up in the ocean where marine animals mistake them for food and eat them.

• When you visit the beach or park carry out your trash or dispose of it properly in trash containers.

• Reduce waste. Buy jumbo size and products with the least amount of packaging.

• Next time you see trash, pick it up and dispose of it properly.

• Don't dispose anything (car fluids, paint, lawn debris, or trash) down storm drains or roadways that will drain into storm drains.

A special thanks to:

Neil Furukawa
Eddy Gudoy
Ryan Kaminaga
Devon Nekoba
Clint Sekioka